THE ETCHER'S STUDIO

Arthur Geisert

HOUGHTON MIFFLIN COMPANY BOSTON

1 9 9 7

For my father and his father and their garages

Walter Lorraine  Books

Library of Congress Cataloging-in-Publication Data

Geisert, Arthur.
  The etcher's studio / Arthur Geisert.
    p.   cm.
  Summary: As a young boy helps prepare etchings for sale at his
grandfather's studio, he imagines himself as part of some of the
pictures. Includes a description of how etchings are made.
  ISBN 0-395-79754-3
  [1. Etching—Fiction.   2. Artists—Fiction.   3. Imagination—
Fiction.   4. Grandfathers—Fiction.]   I. Title.
PZ7.G2724Et   1997
[E]—dc20   96-35000
                                                      CIP
                                                      AC

For information about this and other Houghton Mifflin trade
and reference books and multimedia products, visit The Bookstore
at Houghton Mifflin on the World Wide Web at
http://www.hmco.com/trade.
Printed in the United States of America
HOR   10   9   8   7   6   5   4   3   2

THE ETCHER'S STUDIO

My grandfather was an etcher. Each year he would have a studio sale.

I helped him get ready.

I unpacked the paper that Grandfather soaked in water to make it soft for printing.

I helped him worry about how long to leave his plate in the acid.

I put wood in the stove while Grandfather inked and wiped his plate.

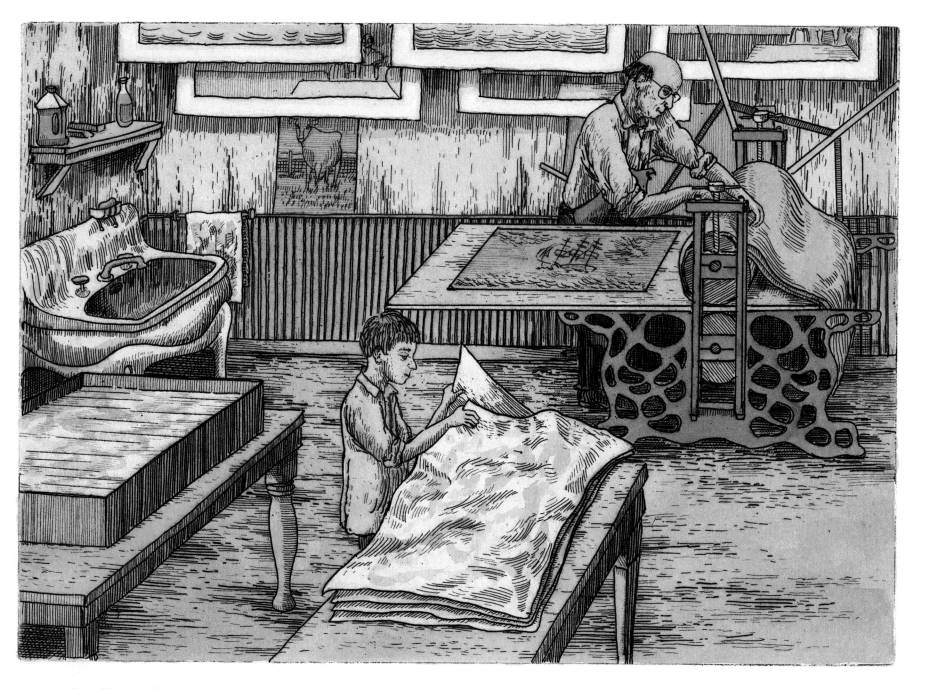

As Grandfather prepared the press, I blotted the wet paper.

When all was ready he turned the wheel, rolling the plate and paper through the press.

The proof looked good.

Then it was time for me to get to work.

My job was to color the prints by hand. It was tedious work and my mind would wander.

I would imagine myself in the pictures.

One afternoon I sailed around Cape Horn.

Another time I flew over our town in a balloon that I was coloring.

I changed places with a deep sea diver.

I explored a jungle.

But I couldn't dream all the time.

I had to concentrate to get the colors right on the print.

After weeks of work, the prints were finally ready for the sale.

Grandfather congratulated me on a job well done.

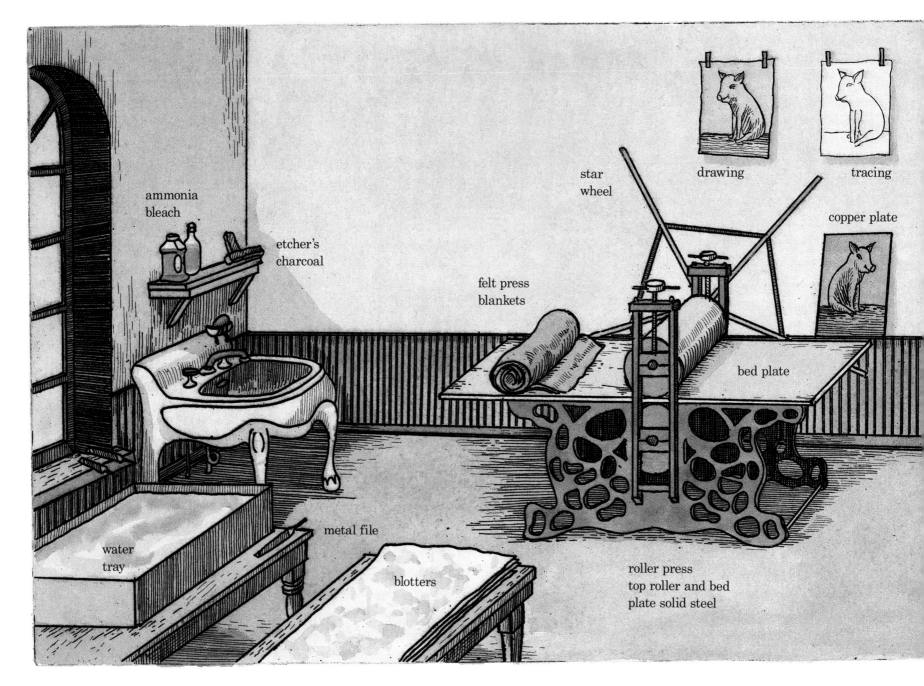

ammonia
bleach

etcher's
charcoal

star
wheel

drawing

tracing

copper plate

felt press
blankets

bed plate

metal file

water
tray

blotters

roller press
top roller and bed
plate solid steel

An Etcher's Studio

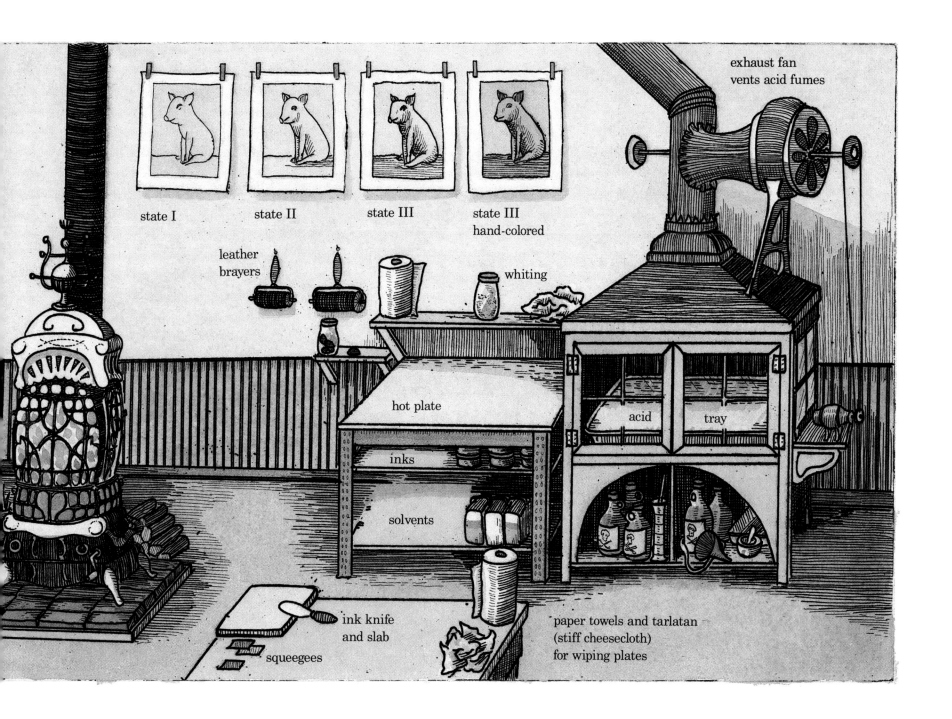

state I

state II

state III

state III
hand-colored

exhaust fan
vents acid fumes

leather
brayers

whiting

hot plate

inks

solvents

acid   tray

ink knife
and slab

squeegees

paper towels and tarlatan
(stiff cheesecloth)
for wiping plates

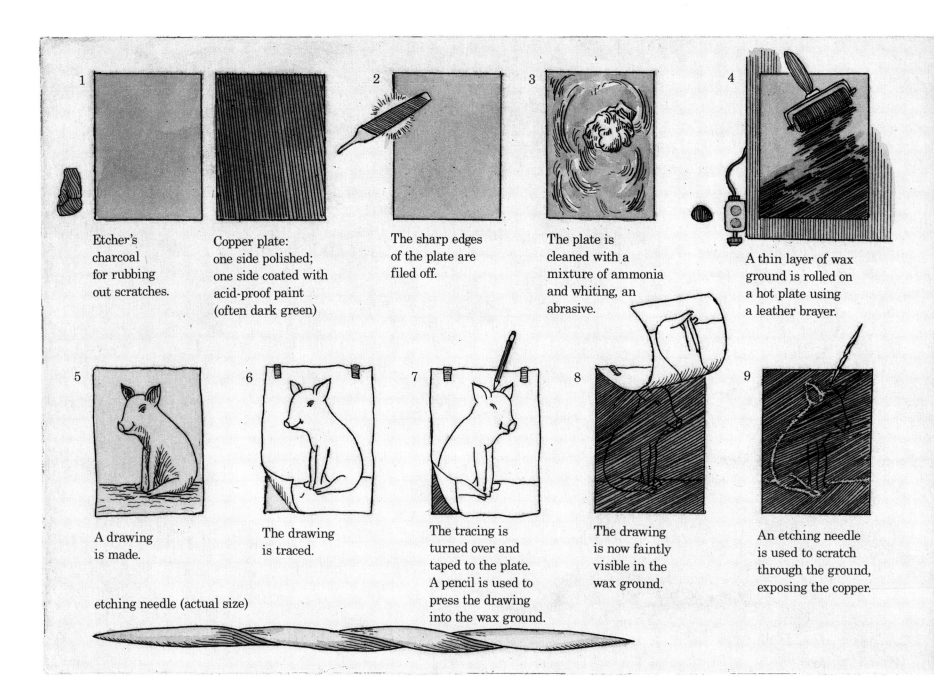

1. Etcher's charcoal for rubbing out scratches.

Copper plate: one side polished; one side coated with acid-proof paint (often dark green)

2. The sharp edges of the plate are filed off.

3. The plate is cleaned with a mixture of ammonia and whiting, an abrasive.

4. A thin layer of wax ground is rolled on a hot plate using a leather brayer.

5. A drawing is made.

etching needle (actual size)

6. The drawing is traced.

7. The tracing is turned over and taped to the plate. A pencil is used to press the drawing into the wax ground.

8. The drawing is now faintly visible in the wax ground.

9. An etching needle is used to scratch through the ground, exposing the copper.

How an Etching Is Made

10

The plate
ready to etch.

11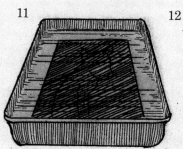

Acid eats or etches
into the exposed lines
of the plate. The acid
is hydrochloric with
potassium chlorate.

12

The ground is removed
with mineral spirits,
leaving the etched line
clearly visible. The
plate is ready to print.

13

Thick, sticky ink
is smeared over
the entire plate,
using a mattboard
squeegee.

14

The plate is
wiped with paper
towels and tarlatan.
Ink remains in the
lines.

15

roller press

felt press
blankets

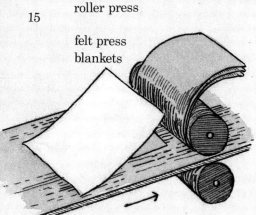

Paper soaked in water with
a touch of bleach is blotted
and placed on the inked and
wiped plate. The felts go
over the paper.

16

The pressure of
the press
pushes the paper
into the inked
lines.

17

The plate is
regrounded and more
lines are drawn. After
another acid "bite,"
another proof
is pulled.

18

The process
is repeated
for a third
time.

19

The third
proof, hand-
colored.

Since the beginning of time man has scratched, etched, and engraved various materials with a fundamental urge for self-expression. Metal was etched and engraved centuries before anybody thought of inking and printing the designs. It wasn't until paper became available in the Western world that etchings appeared as we know them today. The earliest etchings date from the late fifteenth century. In the past five hundred years little has changed in technique. Though iron and steel presses have replaced wooden presses and electric and gas hot plates have replaced charcoal braziers, the inks, grounds, tools, acid, and paper remain the same. Not all etchings are hand-colored. In the past, hand-coloring was traditionally a young apprentice's work.

The illustrations for this book were etched on copper and were hand-colored. The technique, tools, and equipment used were almost identical to what is shown in this book.